DAGMAR SCHULTZ AND THE ANGEL EDNA

Other Books by Lynn Hall

DAGMAR SCHULTZ
AND THE
ANGEL
EDNA

LYNN HALL

CHARLES SCRIBNER'S SONS
NEW YORK

Charles Scribner's Sons Books for Young Readers
Macmillan Publishing Company
866 Third Avenue, New York, NY 10022
Collier Macmillan Canada, Inc.

Printed in the United States of America
First Edition   10 9 8 7 6 5 4 3 2 1

Library of Congress Cataloging-in-Publication Data
Hall, Lynn.
    Dagmar Schultz and the angel Edna/Lynn Hall.
—1st ed.   p.   cm.
(Charles Scribner's Sons Books for Young Readers)
    Summary: Boy-crazy thirteen-year-old Dagmar fi-
nally locates potential romance in her quiet Iowa com-
munity, only to find herself the special project of a
guardian angel with very old-fashioned morals.
[1. Guardian angels—Fiction.   2. Angels—Fiction.
3. Iowa—Fiction.   4. Humorous stories.]
I. Title.   II. Series
PZ7.H1458Dae 1989   [Fic]—dc19
88–36862 CIP   AC   ISBN 0–684–19097–4

DAGMAR SCHULTZ AND THE ANGEL EDNA

One

I've got enough trouble in my life. I really don't need Edna.

You might think I have a pretty good life if you just look at things on the surface. I'm young and healthy and on the verge of turning gorgeous. I've got beautiful long hair that I can almost sit on if I hang my head way back till my neck cracks. My figure is coming along pretty well for my age; better than my girlfriend Shelly's anyhow, and that's all that matters.

My parents love me and each other, and I live in a pretty nice little town in northeast Iowa, where everybody knows who I am and who all my ancestors were. I'm smart enough to get by in school

1

without having to throw up in the rest room before tests like one boy in our class does.

So you're probably saying to yourself, "Dagmar Schultz has it made. What's she bellyaching about? The world is full of people worse off than she is."

Well, that's true, but on the other hand, my problems are more important to me than anybody else's, and this is my story, so are you going to listen or not? I haven't got to the good part yet.

My point is that even though my life might look pretty good on the surface, it's not a bed of rosebuds, believe me.

First, there's my family. My dad is all right. He's real old, and kind of small and wiry and silly. He likes to do things like popping his false teeth out when you're not expecting it. Daddy's kind of a town handyman. He loves me a lot, and he's fun to kid around with.

Mom is okay, too, except she's real fat, and that can be embarrassing sometimes, like when she comes to school for Parents' Night. I try to act as if it doesn't matter what the other kids say about her, but it does, a little bit. She doesn't usually come to Parents' Night, though. She'd rather stay home with the baby. She loves babies and kind of loses interest in us after we get past the baby stage.

I'm the oldest and best of the kids, if I do say so myself. Below me there's my brother Cootie, my show-off sister GeorgeAnn (you wouldn't like her), and then the boys, David and Deaney. And the baby, Delight, who isn't old enough to be much trouble to me.

I have to share a room with GeorgeAnn, so she's the worst because she's always staring at me, especially when I get undressed. Cootie used to drive me nuts, too, but now he's eleven and he's got his own bunch of friends that he's always off doing things with.

Actually, the worst of the relatives are all the uncles and aunts and cousins and grandparents. They act as if I'm their personal property and every private little corner of my life is open for discussion. Last week my Gramma Schultz told Daddy he should make me quit wearing a bra. She said back in her day girls my age didn't wear bras. Girls in her day must have flopped a lot, that's all I can say.

And my Cousin Neese (short for Denise) acts as if she knows everything just because she's sixteen and her mother has a beauty shop. She might know more about eye makeup than I do, but she was the one who told me anybody with a hickey is pregnant, and that's not true. Of course, she was only twelve when she told me that. She knows better now. But she's always making comments, like telling me it's time to shave under my arms. Neese has real fat hips, so her legs look knock-kneed, and her hair is just one big pile of frizz.

The other main problem in my life besides lack of privacy is . . . lack of boyfriend. My best friend, Shelly, got the only boy our age in New Berlin.

That's our town. Pronounced BERlin, like Merlin. Don't ask me why.

Anyhow, Shelly beat me to him, mainly because I didn't want him all that much. Matthew isn't too bad looking, but he's dumber than a brick, and all he cares about is his four-wheeler. Shelly is willing to make a fool of herself riding around town with Matthew on the back of his four-wheeler, hugging and squealing like a stuck hog. That kind of stuff is beneath my dignity.

But I really do want a boyfriend. There's this boy James who rides my bus, and he's kind of neat. For a while I was in love with him, but all he cares about is basketball and his farm. The trouble with boys my age is that they aren't my age! It's so frustrating.

So you can see why my life was not a bed of rosebuds, even before Edna came along.

One of the main things I'd been dying for, I finally did get. My thirteenth birthday. Twelve is such a stupid age to be, and twelve felt as if it lasted about twenty years. But finally, last week, the magic day arrived: November ninth.

It was a Thursday, so the birthday party wasn't as big as it would have been on a weekend, but that was fine with me since it was all relatives except for Shelly. Neese was there, of course, with her parents, Uncle Dean and Aunt Dorothy. Then there was Uncle Martin and Aunt Bev from Littleport, and Gramma Schultz from the Lutheran

Retirement Home in Strawberry Point, and another aunt-uncle family from over by Clayton Center. And Aunt Gretchen.

I like Aunt Gretchen, when she isn't causing me actual pain. She's Mom's sister, Built like a tugboat, Daddy says. She's a bookkeeper at the Happy Auto Body Shop, and she's the best pitcher in the women's softball league, not to mention being the star of her bowling league. She does a little more belly punching and hair pulling than I like, but at least she doesn't try to run my life quite as much as the rest of them do.

People started driving up after supper, and by eight you could hardly find floor space to step onto. Our house is pretty good sized, a big, old, square place painted different colors on different sides because Daddy never seems to finish a paint job. But it's been that way so long that no one in town even notices anymore.

The party was about like all our family birthday parties. Mom and Aunt Gretchen shoved the dining-room table over against one wall and covered it with dishes of salted nuts and baloney wrapped around asparagus, big bowls of chips and dip, and another big bowl of Kool-Aid punch. The older people sat on the living-room chairs and sofa, the not-so-old people sat on the floor, and the little kids played in the middle. David and Deaney ran their toy race cars up people's legs, and Delight took little tottering steps from one set of hands to another. Sixteen different people lifted her lip to feel where her new teeth were coming in.

You can see how thrilling birthday parties are in the Schultz family.

Of course everybody gave me a hug or a pat when they came in, and told me how tall I'd gotten since the last time they saw me, and asked how it felt to be a teenager. It would have been great if they'd all brought presents, but our family is too big for everybody to give to everybody, so mostly it was just cards and pats and "how does it feel to be a teenager?" and then on to feeling Delight's new teeth and talking about boring stuff that had nothing to do with me.

When everybody was present and accounted for, Mom brought out the cake from the kitchen, and we sang happy birthday to me, and I did all the corny blowing-out-of-candles stuff.

"What did you wish?" Cootie demanded.

"Don't tell, Hair," Aunt Gretchen bellowed across the room. "If you tell, it won't come true."

"She wished for a boyfriend," GeorgeAnn said in her taunting voice. She was mad because she'd been playing her recital piece on the piano, "Twinkling Stars," and nobody even noticed over the roar of voices. Generally she can play louder than any human voice, but this was quite a herd of Schultzes all packed into one living room and dining room.

Of course she'd hit the nail right on the thumb, guessing that I wished for a boyfriend.

Obviously there wasn't going to be a boyfriend in any of the packages on the coffee table, but I tore into them with some excitement anyhow. There is just something about an unopened present with your name on it—the wild hope that it will be something wonderful, or at least something you can use.

It didn't start out too great: a clay ashtray that GeorgeAnn made at school. I really needed an ashtray. Then some gold seashell earrings from Cootie. They still had the K Mart sale-price sticker on the back of the cardboard. Three ninety-eight. Daddy won't let me pierce my ears, so I couldn't wear them. But it was nice to have them anyhow, for later.

From Mom and Daddy, a dress and two skirts that Mom made, which were pretty nice, and a beautiful pair of white satin slippers with wedge heels, like a movie star would wear to lounge around her penthouse. I loved them. I could tell Daddy picked them out for me because they were so impractical and so perfect for me.

Uncle Dean and family gave me a neat pink plastic portable radio, one of those little ones that you hang on your belt and listen to through tiny earphones.

"Be careful of the volume," Aunt Dorothy said.

"You can damage your eardrums with those things."

Then why did you give it to me, I wondered, but I didn't say it out loud.

Aunt Gretchen gave me a gift pack of cologne, bath powder, and hand lotion. White Shoulders, the scent was called. I loved it.

Shelly gave me three pairs of pantyhose and a paperback teen romance novel that she'd already read. I could tell by the creases down its back. At least the pantyhose weren't secondhand. Probably. I checked the seal on each package, just to be sure.

By ten o'clock most of them were gone, all but Uncle Dean and family, and Aunt Gretchen. Mom put Delight and the boys down for the night, and by the time she came back we'd dragged the dining-room table back into the middle of the room, hauled its chairs into place, and shoved the leftover food into the middle of the table, to make room for arms and elbows and beer for the men and Aunt Gretchen.

I had something important to ask Daddy, but it didn't look as if the rest of the company was about to leave, so I just slouched down on the piano bench and waited for a break in the conversation. By spreading my arms out over the keyboard behind me, I managed to head off GeorgeAnn's attempts to play.

"Daddy," I said.

"If you ask me," he said, "we're better off without it. Not nearly so much traffic these days, and those big noisy trucks can't get through town at all. For my money they can leave that bridge just like it is till doomsday."

I sighed. The great bridge controversy. They could be on that subject for hours. The Volga River runs through the middle of New Berlin, and it's got two bridges across it, the old one in the middle of town and the new one out at the edge of town, on the highway. A while back somebody found cracks in the old bridge and they closed it. Then nobody could decide whether the town or the county actually owned it, and neither one of them wanted to pay to fix it or replace it. So it's been closed for about four weeks now. You can walk across it, but to drive from one side of town to the other you have to go around by the highway. Big deal. I liked it closed, myself. Somebody put a basketball hoop up on one end, at the top of the Keep Off the Bridge sign, so now on Saturday afternoons there's always a bunch of guys down there shooting baskets. They're talking about putting a hoop at the other end and having regular games. The only trouble is, they've already lost four balls that went over the railing and floated downstream.

"Daddy," I said again a half hour later when they got tired of talking bridge and the silences were getting long enough to be boring.

"What, old lady?" He swung around in his chair and grabbed me by the ankle. I'd been propping my feet against the back of his chair.

"Now that I'm thirteen, can I go out on dates?"

The room got quiet for a split second. Then Cootie let out a hoot and pointed at me, laughing his stupid head off. GeorgeAnn joined in with him and tackled him, and they went rolling across the living-room floor screeching, "Dagmar wants to go out on dates. Who'd go out on a date with her? She's so ugly she makes me throw up."

Cootie stuck his finger down his throat and made sickening sounds.

Meanwhile Aunt Dorothy and Mom were laughing and smiling their wise-older-woman smiles at each other. Neese was cackling and Uncle Dean was hoo-hawing like I'd told a joke. I didn't see what was so funny.

Aunt Gretchen looked at me as if she thought I was nuts. Only Daddy took me seriously. That is, he managed to fight back a grin and pretend he was taking me seriously.

"Who'd you have in mind, if I may ask?" he asked.

"Well, nobody exactly." I was getting all red in the face, and I hated them for watching me. "What I meant was, if I should get a boyfriend, would you let me go out on dates, now that I'm in my teens?"

The room got totally quiet. That was almost worse than the hoo-hawing. Daddy shifted clear around in his chair and sort of looked me up and down as if he'd never seen me before.

"That's a fair question and it deserves a serious answer," he said.

"So?"

"So let me think about this for a minute. Thirteen is still awful young, you know."

I heaved a huge sigh. Thirteen was the prize I had won for spending ten years being twelve. It seemed like ten years anyhow. Now here he was telling me I still hadn't gotten anywhere.

"Well?" I said after a long, silent pause.

"It would depend," Daddy finally stated in his heavy-father voice.

"On what?"

"On getting a boyfriend," Cootie yelled, and he and GeorgeAnn went back to wrestling and whooping on the living-room floor.

"On who the young man was," Daddy said carefully.

"We'd have to know him and his family," Uncle Dean chimed in. Who asked him?

"You couldn't go out alone with a boy in his car," Daddy said. "Anybody old enough to have a license would be too old for you. So it couldn't be a car date."

He thought some more.

"You couldn't go alone with a boy," he said slowly. "Not that I wouldn't trust you; I wouldn't trust any boy your age. And you couldn't go with a

11

group. Too much chance for reckless driving, or drinking or drugs or that kind of thing."

I sighed.

"You couldn't go anyplace very far, or very late. I would have to drive you and bring you home. And I wouldn't want you being alone with this boy."

I rolled my eyes toward heaven, as if I expected some help from there.

Then Daddy smiled. "Within those little guidelines, sure, honey. You can have all the dates you want."

Wonderful, wonderful.

I gathered an armload of birthday presents and plomped up the stairs toward my room.

"Happy birthday," they all yelled at me from down below.

The big one-three had arrived . . . and Edna was about to.

Two

Sometimes my mind gets so full of excitement it won't turn itself off and let me get to sleep. I lay on my bed after the birthday party, just thinking up a storm. Not under the covers, because I didn't want to take off the sexy satin slippers with the wedge heels yet. They probably looked funny with my jeans, but who cared? They made me feel beautiful and mature.

GeorgeAnn flopped around on her bed for a long time, snorting and kicking one leg up over the covers, and sending as much irritating noise as possible across the chalk line that divided her half of the room from mine. But finally she zonked off to sleep and I had the place to myself.

Besides the slippers, I also wore the pink plastic

portable radio, hooked onto my belt and riding on top of my stomach, with the tiny little earphones in my ears. The local radio station at Elkader was playing country-western oldies from back in the sixties and seventies. It wasn't my favorite kind of music, but apparently little pink radios don't reach very far. It was the only station I could get.

I wasn't thinking about the music anyhow. I was thinking about being thirteen years old at long last, and having permission to date. Well, if you could call it permission. Can't go in a car, can't go alone or with anyone, has to be a boy that everyone in my huge family knows and approves of.

But still, my foot was in the door, and the more I thought about it, the more excited and unsleepy I got. All I had to do now was find a boyfriend and get him to ask me for a date. And decide what to wear.

And have Neese figure out something spectacular to do with my hair and my eye makeup.

I could wear my black top with the sequinned dragon all across the front. That was an eye-catcher. Maybe tight black velvet pants with a sash around the waist. High heels. Really high spike heels.

I was mentally reviewing every boy I knew at school when the radio announcer did his sign-off speech.

"This concludes the day's broadcast from KADR, Elkader, Iowa, in the heart of the hill country."

And then something about watts and channels.

Then static. I was fumbling for the on-off button on the radio when I heard a woman's voice, sort of far off and faint, coming through the static.

"Dagmar Schultz, is that you?"

I shook my head a little, to clear it, and pulled the earphones away from my head. Silence through the house, except for Mom's snoring from their bedroom downstairs.

I waited a long time, thinking someone must be calling me.

"Dagmar Schultz, can you hear me? Put the earphones back on, dear."

I sat straight up, stared down at the earphones in my hand, and gingerly put them on again.

"There now, that's better, isn't it, dear?" It was definitely a voice talking to me, a sort of middle-aged motherly kind of voice, and it was much clearer. But where the heck was it coming from? The radio station had signed off for the night. And how could someone be talking to me personally, through a radio?

"Can you hear me, dear?" the voice said sweetly.

I nodded. I didn't know what else to do. Talk about feeling like a fool!

"This is your Aunt Edna speaking to you," the voice said. "I've been trying to get through to you for weeks now, but it's been so difficult. You just can't imagine what I've been through. I almost

15

made it last Thursday night, or was it Friday? No, no, I believe it was Thursday. Do you remember, dear? You were talking to your little friend Sally on the telephone, and I called your name just as you were hanging up, do you remember?"

"Who *are* you?" I demanded.

"This is your Aunt Edna. I just told you. Young people today certainly don't pay attention the way they used to. You hung up the telephone right in my ear, too. That was quite rude, you know."

I thought back to last Thursday, as well as I was capable of thinking when I had no idea what was going on or where this voice was coming from.

"Her name is Shelly, not Sally," I said. "I remember talking to her, but I don't remember you butting in. Lots of times you can hear other people's voices in the background, if you have a bad connection. I probably just thought you were a bad connection. Who *are* you?"

GeorgeAnn snuffled and snorted and thrashed around, as if she was threatening to wake up.

"I don't *have* an Aunt Edna," I whispered nastily. "I have every other kind of aunt in the world, but I'm sure I don't have an Aunt Edna, and where is your voice coming from?"

"From Beyond," she said. "Well, of course we don't call it that. Here, it's just plain Level Three, but it's what you might call Beyond. And actually I'm your father's great-aunt, Edna Halverson. I was a Bolls before I was married. Henry Bolls was

16

my father. From Strawberry Point. Well, our home place was over closer to Maryville, but Maryville isn't even there anymore, just a truck stop and the big creamery, but it used to be quite a busy—"

"Who *cares*," I yelled.

GeorgeAnn sat up and glared at me through the dark. She can do that. "Shut up, Dagmar, or I'm telling Mom."

"Sorry," I muttered. "I was having a bad dream."

When she'd zonked off again I whispered, "You are a bad dream, aren't you, Aunt Edna?"

"Why no, dear. Actually I'm your guardian angel."

I caught myself just before I yelled out loud again. "My what?"

"Now, I know the idea may take a little getting used to, dear. Goodness knows it took me quite a while to understand the system when they explained it to me. Just in a general way, what happens is that everyone on Level One, which is where you are—that is, you're what *you* call 'alive.'"

A cold hand of fear clutched my heart. I'm not just saying that. It really did.

The voice went on. "Everyone on Level One has a spirit guide, what you'd call a guardian angel. It's usually a relative or someone close like that, someone with a genuine personal interest, don't you know. I mean, it just wouldn't be the same watching over someone you hardly knew, would it?"

This was a dead person talking to me through my radio headphones, or I was totally insane and ready for the looney bin.

". . . told the chairman of the spirit guide committee—Rudy his name is—'Rudy,' I said to him, 'I don't think I'm ready for this duty yet.' But he said, 'Now Eddie,'—he always calls me Eddie." She giggled. "'You'll do just fine, Eddie. You always have. And you died a hero's death, don't forget. So you just pick out the guidee you want and get to work.' That's what Rudy told me to do, so I picked you. Actually I asked for Wendell Pickard. Do you know him? Lovely little boy, lives over in Illinois. Jim and Elvadene Pickard's youngest boy. I had boys, myself, and I was always glad. Boys are so much easier to raise than girls, don't you think?"

"Who *cares*," I whispered again through gritted teeth. "What I want to know is, who are you really and how did you get tapped into this radio?"

The voice gave a very long, patient sigh. "Rudy warned me not to try to make direct contact. He said it always leads to confusion because so few people are open-minded enough to accept the fact that there are spirit guides. SGs, we call ourselves for short. We have a little social club. Well, not little. There are quite a lot of us, don't you know. But we have little local groups, nice Wednesday-night get-togethers to compare problems we're

18

having with our guidees. Once a month it's a pot-luck dinner."

"Okay, okay," I said. "I'll play along with your silly game. Okay, you're a dead person talking to me through my radio headphones, right? You're my dead great-aunt Edna, and you're going to be my guardian angel."

"No, no, dear. You weren't paying attention. I'd be your great-great-aunt. Henry Bolls was my father, and my sister married Lionel Schultz, who was your—"

"Just get on with it." My teeth were so gritted I thought my jaw was locked.

"Well, Dagmar dear, I'm trying to explain, but you do interrupt a good deal, don't you. Haven't your parents taught you any better manners than that? Never mind, you have me now. As I started to say, Rudy always advises against making direct contact with our guidees. He prefers more subtle guardianship, like shaking a dozing driver by the nape of the neck just before the car goes into the ditch, or making you remember you left the oven on before the house catches fire. That sort of thing. Putting ideas into heads or taking them out again."

"Uh-huh," I said. I was beginning to believe what I was hearing. I couldn't believe I was believing it, but she sounded so . . . reasonable.

"Okay, Aunt Edna," I said cautiously, "so you picked me out to be your . . ."

"Guidee."

19

"Guidee. How come? And why are you making, uh, direct contact?"

"Well, dear, they wouldn't let me have the little Pickard boy, and you were the only one in the family who was the right age. And of course, I'd been watching you for quite some time now, and it was plain as a pikestaff, you needed more guarding than average. You are what we used to call boy crazy in my day, Dagmar."

The voice sounded so disapproving that suddenly I was convinced. This was so typical of my luck! I couldn't even get away from the million watching eyes of my family *after* they died. There was not only a whole county full of assorted relatives watching me down here, there was also, apparently, an entire heaven, or Level Three, or whatever, full of my aunts and uncles watching every move I made.

I was sure as heck doomed to be a virgin.

I could just see myself in bed with my husband or lover or whatever, and there would be Aunt Edna and the heavenly hosts looking down and saying, "Tut tut, Dagmar. Naughty naughty."

"To get to the point," Aunt Edna said, "you have me, now, to help you through life's little rough spots, and to help you achieve your goals. I just wanted to let you know that."

Achieve goals? Suddenly I began to see some hope in the situation.

20

"Hey, Aunt Edna, could you help me get something I really, really want?"

"Of course, my child. We SGs can do anything we want. Well, within reason. I did want to win that last gin rummy tournament—"

I interrupted, fast. "Could you help me get a boyfriend?"

There was a moment of silence, then Aunt Edna said, "No, no, Dagmar dear. No boyfriend. You are much too young and foolish. No boyfriend. No, not until you are old enough."

"How old do I have to be?" I asked darkly.

'Hmm, hmmm. Let me think. I'd say about . . . twenty."

I ripped the headphones off, pulled them out of the radio, turned the radio off, and stuffed it under the bed.

Three

Try taking an American history test right after you've had your first conversation with a dead aunt. If you think it's possible to concentrate on the dates of the industrial revolution at a time like that, you're crazy.

So of course we had a surprise test the next morning, and I flunked it. "Thanks a lot, guardian angel," I muttered as I slouched out of the classroom, hiding inside my hair. Whenever I want to disappear off the face of the earth from embarrassment, I let my hair swing forward like curtains around my face and just hide in it. I don't know what kids with short hair do for a hiding place. Hunch up their shoulders, I guess.

"Tough luck on that test," said a boy's voice behind me as I trudged up the hall toward English.

I turned around and looked into the sympathetic face of Aron Bodensteiner. He sat behind me in history, and he'd heard my grade.

"Thanks," I said. "I just wasn't concentrating."

"Yeah, Fridays I can never concentrate either," Aron said with a fairly friendly smile and faded off into the crowd.

Hmmm, I thought. Aron Bodensteiner. A possibility. Yes, he could be boyfriend material. I added him to the list of candidates in my mind as I slipped into my seat in English just before the bell rang.

For the rest of the day I concentrated on not screwing up in any more of my classes, but in between times I kept scanning the halls and classrooms for likely boyfriends. Not that I hadn't been doing this all year, of course, but now that I had semipermission to have dates, the hunt was on full force.

Naturally, I was going to be pretty darned fussy. I was Dagmar Schultz, after all, and Dagmar Schultz was a potential knock-'em-dead gorgeous chick. Okay, so I wasn't quite there yet, but I was getting closer all the time. A little more shape to the bod, a little less baby fat around the cheeks, a little sexier look in the eye. Any boy in eighth grade, or even ninth grade, would be darned lucky to get me.

The trick was finding a boy who was smart enough to know that.

He'd have to be smart enough to appreciate me, and he'd have to be cute enough to rank above gross level. I mean, there were some boys that if they were known as your boyfriends, you'd never live it down.

So my candidates had to be smart enough to appreciate me, cute enough to be good catches, nice enough for me to enjoy being with them. And they had to be connected with me in some way, so I could chase them without their knowing it, like arranging to be getting on the bus at the same time. Stuff like that.

During lunch hour I started a list, on the back page in my notebook, of all the possible possibilities. And all afternoon I scratched off one name after another. Too stuck-up. Too interested in some other girl. Too dumb, or too smart, or too hard to make contact with.

By the beginning of last period every name on the list was blacked out, except Aron Bodensteiner. And then I knew I'd been cheating a teeny bit on myself, finding reasons to scratch the rest of them off because deep down I really wanted it to be Aron.

My heart turned a couple of flip-flops inside my ribs, and I knew I was in love. I recognized the feeling, because I'd felt it last month for James Mann, but I'd finally dumped him because all he could think of was basketball. He passed up lots of chances to flirt with me, therefore he didn't deserve me and I dumped him. He probably didn't realize he'd been dumped, but it sure made me feel better.

My last class was algebra, but on Friday afternoons Mr. Hartung just gave us our weekend assignment and let us use class time to start on it. He was the boys' track coach and didn't care any more about algebra than the rest of us. We were all just going through the motions so he wouldn't lose his coaching job. We understood that and tried to help him out by getting passing grades, because we all liked him.

But it wasn't the kind of class you actually have to pay attention in, at least not on Fridays, when mentally Mr. Hartung wasn't in the room, either. His mind was out in the stadium blowing a whistle and yelling "Pump those legs."

So I had plenty of time to think about Aron, my new true love.

He had lots going for him. For one thing, he was tall, and in eighth grade half the boys were shorter than I am. He was tall and kind of broad shouldered, although he was still skinny around the chest. He looked like he'd turn into a real hunk when he got all his chest and arm muscles, and I could wait.

He was homely-cute in the face, with black-rimmed glasses and front teeth that kind of folded sideways across each other. Dark hair, hazel eyes, skin a mess, but I could outwait the pimples, too.

If we ended up getting married, the face would be fine by that time.

There were two important points in his favor: He hadn't shown any noticeable amount of interest in any other girls, and he had a connection with me. He lived on a farm out on Holstein Dip Road, not too far from New Berlin. He was on a different bus route from me, but his farm's rear end was up against the rear end of Uncle Dean's farm, which was on the quarry road.

The Volga River ran alongside both farms, and both farms had big stretches of timber along the river, adjoining each other without even a line fence in between, so the whole hundred acres of timber was one big Happy Hunting Ground. Around the middle of May, people would drive out from town and walk into Bodensteiners' timber, hunting morel mushrooms. Those are the ones that look like big sponges on a stalk, and are they ever good! You soak them in salt water to get the ants out, and then you slice them, roll them in cracker crumbs, and fry them in butter.

Then in the fall, around late October, town people drive out again and go ginseng hunting in the woods, because you can sell the dried ginseng root to a buyer in Dubuque for fifty dollars a pound.

In between mushroom season and ginseng season the woods are more private, but Daddy and Uncle Dean and Aron's dad have gone together, some years, and run trap lines along the river. Last winter Daddy and Uncle Dean took my brother Cootie back there squirrel hunting several times. And I remember one time Aron was out there hunting, too, and went along with them for a while.

So, with a little effort on my part, it shouldn't be too hard to manage to run across Aron sometime in the woods. It would be natural enough for me to be there, and I'd be sure to be ready for him— freshly shampooed hair, a little of the birthday cologne, maybe a twisted ankle so he'd have to put his arm around me and help me home.

What the heck, it always worked in the romance novels.

I decided I'd better make my move right away. Eighth grade was full of girls all trying to get a jump on the competition, and it was a safe bet that I wasn't the only one who had seen Aron's potential.

The bell finally rang. Mr. Hartung waved us off and practically beat us out the door himself.

As I charged into the hall with the flow of traffic, I had a brief uncomfortable thought. Aunt Edna. I'd managed to push her to the back of my mind during most of the day, because I was concentrating on the boyfriend list.

Now she was suddenly in my thoughts, so clearly that I wondered if she was broadcasting to me. Nah, just my imagination, I decided.

I wasn't exactly sure where Aron's locker was,

but instinct for the hunt led me to the area between the boys' rest room and the science lab, and bingo!

He was standing in front of his opened locker, more or less alone, and shuffling through his books and notebooks, maybe deciding what he'd need to take home for the weekend.

Think fast, I told myself. My mind was a total blank, but I went up to him and opened my mouth anyhow, hoping something intelligent would come out.

"Hi, Aron."

He looked around, saw me, acted neither thrilled nor unthrilled, just sort of normal.

"Hi, Dagmar."

"Got a big weekend planned?" I asked. I sounded so cool and casual I wanted to pat myself on the back.

He shrugged and tossed a book into the locker. "Getting in the last of the corn tomorrow, if the weather holds," he said. "Maybe a little squirrel hunting Sunday."

"Lots of squirrels this year?" I asked, just as if I gave a rat's tail.

"Yeah," he said. "The woods are full of 'em. Tell Cootie to come on over Sunday if he wants. He can go out with me."

"I will." I tossed my hair and gave him a long, deep, womanly look, eyeball to eyeball.

He kind of turned toward me and faltered a little

bit, as if I was making him dizzy. I'd never felt so powerful in my life as I did right then. Turning thirteen was fantastic!

All of a sudden, while we were standing there making hundred-volt eye contact, his head disappeared.

With a terrible clanging crash, his whole locker tilted forward and fell over onto him. His head disappeared inside, books rained down all over him, and the locker came to rest at a silly angle, held up by Aron with his head inside it.

His arms dropped to his side, and he just stood there like a fence post.

I started to say, "Are you okay?" but halfway through I broke out laughing and in about two seconds there were fifty kids all gathered around, helping to get him out from under but also laughing themselves to death. Well, it did look funny.

As the locker came away from his head, I reached out and caught his glasses on their way to the floor. As I handed them back, I took a good look at him.

He was grinning. Whew. I liked him ten times more than I had before, knowing he had a good sense of humor.

"I'm sorry," I said. "I didn't mean to laugh. It just looked so funny there for a minute. Are you sure you're okay?"

He had a scrape along one side of his nose, and he was rubbing a rising goose egg on the back of his head, but other than that he swore he was fine.

"I just can't figure out how that locker came loose like that," he muttered as he cautiously shoved his books and gym bag back inside it and slammed the door.

The other kids wandered off, and the janitor came clanking up with his belt full of tools. He loved moments like this, when he got to be the star of the drama.

"Toggle bolt's worked loose out of the wall back there," he pronounced, like a doctor on a soap opera.

"Well, see ya," Aron said, and headed toward the south door where the buses were lined up.

"See ya," I called faintly after him.

Toggle bolt just happened to work loose, huh? Just at that moment, and just that one locker.

"Aunt Edna, I'm going to get you for this," I swore through gritted teeth.

Four

That night I had two wonderful choices of how I could spend my Friday evening. I could go with the rest of the family to GeorgeAnn's piano recital and listen to her play "Twinkling Stars" for the trillionth time, or I could stay home and baby-sit Delight and the boys. I took baby-sitting as the best of the bad choices.

By eight o'clock I had Delight down in her crib and asleep, and I'd made David and Deaney go to bed even though they weren't sleepy yet. I told them they could talk or read or play very quietly for a while, just so they didn't come downstairs and bother me.

I only missed a little of the beginning of *Dallas,*

31

and it wasn't hard to catch up with the story. I was currently in love with Bobby.

"It seems to me you're in love with a great many lads," a voice said from behind me.

I'd been lying on the sofa with the afghan over me and a can of Coke in my hand. At the sound of the voice, I jerked up and spilled half the can of Coke all over myself and the afghan that Gramma Schultz had crocheted all one summer.

Oh, no, I thought, sitting up and turning around.

A strange woman was sitting in Daddy's chair in the far corner of the room, doing some kind of sewing. I was about to ask who she was and how she got in without my hearing her . . . when suddenly I knew. I knew that voice.

"Aunt Edna," I said flatly.

She didn't look up, but gave me a long stare over the top of her little teeny gold-rimmed glasses. She was round and rosy looking, with fat arms and legs ending in dainty, small hands and feet. The feet were in patchwork-cloth slippers and were propped up on Daddy's footstool.

She wore what looked like a long cotton dress, full-skirted and silvery gray and faded, as though it had been washed for years. Her hair was in a gray braid across the top of her head.

"I may not be able to stay long," she said, with a suggestion of whine in her voice. "You have no idea of the effort it takes to break through like this.

But I felt it was necessary, Dagmar, dear. It's obvious to me that you are a very headstrong young lady and hell-bent for destruction, if you'll pardon my strong language. You remind me of a young girl I knew when I was alive. Susan, I think her name was. Sally? Susan. No, no, I'm wrong about that, it was Sarah. Sarah Cummings. Her folks lived out past Holstein Dip, near my Uncle Bert's place. Well, not exactly near Uncle Bert's, it was more like—"

"Who *cares*?" I yelled.

She tucked her chin in and gave me a stern look over the glasses. "If you were my daughter you'd have better manners, young lady. Well, now that you've been assigned to me, I'll see what I can do about your manners. And by the way, sit up straight, child. You'll get round shouldered, slumping like that."

I sat up straight.

"That's better, dear. Now if you would just put that hair of yours into nice tidy braids and wipe that blue stuff off your eyelids. And we really must have a talk about boys, Dagmar. You are much too young to be taking an interest in boys. Just like that flighty Sarah Cummings. You don't want to end up like Sarah Cummings, do you?"

In spite of myself I got curious. "Okay, I bite. What happened to Sarah Cummings?"

The glasses slipped clear down to the point of Aunt Edna's nose. She took a minute to adjust them and then went back to her sewing. She had a man's dark sock, slipped over what looked like a wooden egg with a handle sticking out one end of it. The sock had a hole in the heel, which her needle was closing up by weaving back and forth across the hole, with the wooden egg as a stopper for the needle.

"What is that you're doing?" I asked.

"Darning this sock, of course." She looked at me over the glasses. "Don't tell me your mother hasn't taught you to darn socks yet. Big, strapping thirteen-year-old like you. You should be ashamed. You think you're old enough for boys, and you couldn't even darn their socks for them. Or gut a chicken, I'll bet. Can you gut a chicken, Dagmar?"

I stared at her. "You don't gut chickens, they come sealed in packages. You get a package of drumsticks or breasts or whatever." I was getting a little mad. "And we don't darn socks, we throw them out when they get holes in them. You want to make something out of it?"

We glared at each other for three straight minutes.

Finally I said, "Oh, what the heck. You started to tell me about why I don't want to end up like Sarah What's-her-name."

"Cummings. Those Cummingses were a little on the trashy side anyway, so no one was too surprised at the way Sarah turned out. Well, I shouldn't say that. The Bill Cummings side of the family was all right. Bill and his dad ran that old creamery that used to be up there on Chicken Ridge—"

"Who *cares?*" I sputtered again.

"Well, you did ask," Aunt Edna put in primly.

I ground my back teeth. From what little I knew about guardian angels, this one just wasn't hacking it.

"Sarah Cummings rode home from the grange dance all alone with Marvin Slagle," she said, her words weighted with importance.

"Good for her. So what happened?"

"He had to marry her, that's what." Aunt Edna bit off her thread with a quick savage motion.

I turned farther around on the sofa and wrapped the afghan more cozily around my shoulders and knees. This was getting interesting.

"You mean she got knocked up?"

"Beg pardon?" Aunt Edna looked confused.

"You know. Pregnant. Did she have a baby?"

"Oh, no. Oh, my gracious no, it didn't go that far. Oh, my stars and garters, the way you girls talk, it just takes my breath away."

I pondered. "Well, if she wasn't pregnant, how come he had to marry her? And what was so bad about it?"

"Well, my dear child, the girl was compromised! Her reputation was sullied. She had been alone in the dark with a young man for over an hour, in his farm cart. Naturally she had to marry him in order to preserve her reputation. And in later years he turned to . . . drink." Her voice dropped to a whisper on that last word.

I looked wise and nodded. "Boy, life really was dangerous back then, wasn't it? I mean, some guy offers you a ride home from a dance, and powee, you're stuck for life with a lush."

"So you see why you need me to guide you." She tucked her darning away in a needlepoint bag in the chair beside her and gave me her full attention.

I stared at her with slitted eyes. "Was that you, at school today? Did you dump that locker over on Aron's head?"

She nodded and the glasses slipped half an inch down her nose. "You needed my interference, dear."

"All we were doing was talking," I yelled, waving my arm and spilling more Coke on the afghan. "Who gave you the right to interfere in my life anyhow?"

"Rudy," she said simply. "He is the chairman of the SG committee, after all. Who has a better right? He's also quite a good gin rummy player. And a bit of a sport." Her eyes took on a new gleam. "He's single, too, you know. His wife hasn't died yet, which makes him an unwidower, and fair game. And I believe he might just have a little warm spot in his heart for me. I was quite a beauty in my day, don't you know. And of course I did die a hero's death. That counts for quite a bit, on Level Three."

From the pointed way she said it, I could tell she wanted me to ask her how she died. Oh, well, I thought. Humor the old girl.

"How did you die, Aunt Edna?" I chanted.

She rocked back in Daddy's lounger and stretched her feet, wiggling her toes inside the patchwork slippers.

"I don't like to brag," she said modestly.

Uh-huh, I thought.

"But it was rather a spectacular death. You see, the Rock Island Railroad line ran through our farm. Well, not through it, along one side of it, you might say. Quite dangerous it was, too, in hot dry spells. Those locomotives were forever shooting sparks and setting the grass on fire. I remember the time in the summer of sixty-four—or was it sixty-five? No, it was sixty-four because that was the year my youngest brother tried to slide down the hay rope and nearly ruined himself on the big hook at the bottom of the rope. He would have been twelve that year, so it would have been sixty-four . . ."

"Who *cares*!"

"Yes, well, as I was saying, those trains were a caution, in hot dry weather with all those sparks and whatnot."

"So you died fighting a grass fire, right?"

"No, no, dear. Nothing like that. But I remember the time my brother Elvin's favorite cow
got out onto the track and derailed the morning
milk train. Buttercup, her name was. Lovely cow,
too. I remember we used to sit on her back while
Elvin milked her, and she'd run her rough old
tongue over our bare toes. I cried when she went
to her great reward, that morning on the railroad
track. Engineer cried, too. Derailed four cars
loaded with milk on its way to the creamery. It
made a very smelly mess, let me tell you, when
the sun came up and all that spilt milk began to
curdle. Still, as my mother was fond of saying, no
use crying over spilt milk."

"How did you die?" I growled. I didn't care if I
was speaking ill of the dead, this woman was the
most aggravating storyteller I ever knew.

"Oh, yes. Well, it happened in the winter of
ninety-seven."

"Or eight," I muttered.

"No, no, dear. It was the winter of ninety-seven,
because I had just turned forty, and my husband
had given me a lovely shawl for my birthday gift.
Cream-colored wool, with blue swans woven right
into the wool. My, I hated to part with that shawl.

"Well, as I was saying, the train track ran alongside our farm. My husband and I were farming my
family's place then. There was a railroad bridge
just beyond our pasture. I'd gone out there one

evening rather late, because one of the heifers hadn't come in with the rest of the herd.

"I happened to notice that one of the support posts under the railroad bridge was knocked sideways and the tracks were sagging on that side. Of course, my first thought was to go fetch my husband, but then I realized that the seven-fifty was due through there at any moment.

"I knew I had to get across that bridge and flag down the engineer before he got to the bridge, or the train was sure to wreck when the bridge collapsed. And you must understand, this was no morning milk run."

I nodded, just as if I knew what she was talking about.

"The seven-fifty was a passenger train, and a big one at that. It went from Chicago to Minneapolis, with sometimes as many as a hundred people on board."

"So what did you do?" I was getting caught up in this, despite my better judgment.

"I ran out onto the tracks and started across the bridge. I could hear the train coming from the other side. Louder and louder, closer and closer. My foot caught between the ties and I fell, but I got up again and ran forward, waving my new shawl over my head and praying the engineer would see me in time to stop."

"Did he?" I asked, breathless.

"Yes . . . and no. He saw me, but you know it

takes quite a distance to get those big locomotives stopped. He stopped it just before it got to the bridge, but . . ." She looked sad.

"Creamed you, huh?"

She nodded.

We sat in sympathetic silence for a few minutes, then her head jerked up and she looked at the television screen.

"What about—" I started to say, but she shushed me with a wave of her hand. "Wait till the commercial. Here comes that SueEllen Ewing. Now there's a girl who should have listened to her SG and didn't. Let this be a lesson to you, dear. Just see the trouble she's gotten herself into."

We watched the rest of the program in silence, and when the last commercial came on, Aunt Edna faded away.

Five

Saturday morning I chased GeorgeAnn out of our room and did every bit of my homework for the weekend. I wanted to have my time and my mind free for Aron.

It turned out to be a perfect day outside, perfect for November anyhow, cool but sunny. So after lunch I went outside and wandered down the street to the closed-off bridge. Cootie was down there shooting baskets with Matthew Garms, so of course Shelly was there, too, leaning on the Keep Off the Bridge sign and watching Matthew.

It was rather sickening if you ask me. She didn't really like him. She was only hanging onto him because she got to him before I did and she didn't want me taking him away from her. But it was the humiliation she was thinking about, not Matthew, because, let's face it, Matthew is dumber than a brick.

There were a few other people hanging around, too, along the edge of the bridge, some younger kids and old Charlie, who always shows up when anything is happening around town, even a one-on-one basketball game on the bridge.

I hooked my arms over the Keep Off sign between Shelly and old Charlie and started yelling, "Let him have it, Cootie."

I just said that to get Shelly mad. She gave me a dirty look and started doing cheerleading chants for Matthew.

Old Charlie looked me up and down once, as if he was trying to remember who I was. Then he said, "I never knew you to be on your brother's side in anything, girl. You must be getting smarter than you was."

I gave him a dirty look. "I'm not cheering for Cootie, I'm cheering against Matthew."

Then Shelly gave me an even dirtier look. "You're just so jealous you can't see straight, Dagmar. Everybody knows that, don't they, Charlie? You're just jealous because you don't have a boyfriend."

Charlie muttered, "The mouth that girl's got on her, not likely she ever will get no feller, either."

I stuck my nose in the air and ignored both of

them, but of course what Shelly said was true. I was jealous. Her getting a boyfriend before I did was like telling the world she was better than me. Cuter or sexier or something. If I let myself think about it, it made me almost sick.

I trudged back up the hill to my house and spent the next hour standing in front of the bathroom mirror holding my hair in different shapes to see if any of them made me beautiful.

"If you were any good," I said aloud to Aunt Edna, "you'd fix it so I really was as beautiful as I think I am, and then I'd have boyfriends stacked up like firewood."

There was no answer, but I could imagine what she'd say. Something like, "Looks are only skin deep. Be good and your inner beauty will shine through." Junk like that.

Or else she'd accuse me of only wanting Aron to prove I could get a boyfriend, not because I really liked him for himself. That thought made me stop and stare into the mirror for a long time without seeing anything.

Then slowly I went back to combing my hair. No, that part wasn't true, no matter what Aunt Edna might think. I really honestly liked Aron for himself.

And with a little luck and a whole lot of subtle pushing on my part, tomorrow might be the start of our romance.

*   *   *

We all had to go to church Sunday morning. GeorgeAnn sang in Angel Choir, so of course the whole family always had to go to church, although Cootie and I were the only ones who had to suffer through the service. Delight and the boys got to play in the church nursery, down in the basement.

As long as Cootie and I stood up at the right times and went along with the hymns and responsive readings, Mom and Daddy didn't care if we played hangman during the sermon. That broke up the monotony a little. You know hangman, that game where you think up a word and draw a dash for each letter in the word, and then every time your opponent guesses a letter that's not in the word, you draw one more part of a dead body hanging from a noose, and if you get the whole dead body finished before he guesses the word, you win.

When we played hangman that morning, all the words I gave Cootie had to do with hunting: squirrel, timber, rifle. Subtle things like that. I wanted to get him in a squirrel-hunting mood by afternoon.

We had to quit playing hangman while the Angel Choir sang, though. Daddy nudged me a hard one and made me quit drawing my dead body while GeorgeAnn and the rest of them stood up and sang "For the Beauty of the Skies."

44

I used to think Angel Choir was a ridiculous name for those nine little kids up there, since everybody knew how rotten they were, at least part of the time. But now that I'd met my first actual angel I had a whole different slant on the species. They were human, just like everybody else. Good points and bad points. It was interesting to think about.

After church we went home just long enough to change into comfortable clothes. Then we piled in the pickup with all us kids in the back and drove out to Uncle Dean's for Sunday dinner.

Neese, who had her driver's license now and never let you forget it, drove into Strawberry Point and got Gramma Schultz from the Lutheran Home, and we sat her at the head of the table where she liked to be. She was my great-gramma actually, Daddy and Uncle Dean's gramma, and she used to live in this house and be the boss of it. She still had a habit of telling Aunt Dorothy what she was doing wrong, even though it had been Aunt Dorothy's house for twenty years now.

She never did forgive Aunt Dorothy for turning the downstairs bedroom into the Kut and Kurl Beauty Shop, with a sign out front and everything. She said it was a sin to do that to the dignity of a proud farmhouse.

In a way, I could see her point. Uncle Dean's was one of the best farms in the New Berlin area.

The house was huge and built out of cream-colored blocks of stone, and so was the main dairy barn. Stone houses used to be fairly common around here a hundred years ago when a lot of German and Scandinavian people settled in northeast Iowa. Daddy told me those people built homes to last for hundreds of years, and they built them big enough for several generations to live in them together.

Now generations don't live together anymore, I've noticed. When Uncle Dean's parents took over the farm, Gramma and Grampa Schultz moved to a smaller house at the other end of the land, and then after he died she moved to the nursing home. When Uncle Dean and Aunt Dorothy took over the farm, his parents retired to Florida and bought a condo. In a way I think it's kind of sad that grammas and grampas don't stay on in their own homes.

But on the other hand, if Gramma Schultz had stayed in this house, Aunt Dorothy would never have had the guts to open her beauty shop, and I know there have been some years when the weather was bad for the crops, or the prices dropped or the government screwed up, when it was the beauty shop that brought in their living money.

And to hear Gramma Schultz tell it, they have some pretty high old times there at the Lutheran Home, so maybe it's all for the best.

I was sitting next to Gramma Schultz, where I

could help her dish things out onto her plate. She couldn't hold heavy platters very well.

It occurred to me suddenly that she might have known Aunt Edna. Thinking about that all through the sweet potatoes with marshmallows and the ham with cloves stuck all over it, my curiosity ran away with me.

"Gramma, did you ever know somebody in the family named Edna? Maybe an aunt of yours or something like that?"

Gramma thought. "No, I didn't have any aunts named Edna. You're not thinking of Elvira, are you? There was an Elvira on my mother's side."

"No, Edna. I forget her last name. I guess she would have been on Grampa's side of the family, though, come to think of it. I'm sure it was the Schultzes she was connected to. She died around the eighteen-nineties sometime."

Gramma Schultz gave me a dirty look. "How old do you think I am, anyway, Dagmar? I'm only eighty-eight."

"Eighty-nine," Aunt Dorothy corrected softly. Gramma didn't choose to hear her.

"Well, didn't you ever hear Grampa talk about her, though? An Aunt Edna who died saving a whole bunch of people's lives in a train accident?"

Everyone else tapered off their conversations and plugged into ours.

Daddy said, "Where did you ever hear that, Dagmar?"

"I don't know, somebody said something about it one time." I can be terrifically vague when I need to.

Daddy frowned. "An Aunt Edna who died in a train wreck? No, I think you've got your facts screwed up, there, dumpling."

I did not. I had it right from the horse's mouth, so to speak, but I couldn't tell them that. They thought I was nuts enough as it was. "I do not," I insisted. "Her name was Edna Something, and she was related to the Schultzes and lived up around Holstein Dip somewhere, and she died in the eighteen-nineties, crawling across a railroad bridge over the Volga River to warn the train that the bridge was broken. She got the train stopped in time by waving her shawl with the blue swans on it, but the train couldn't get stopped in time and it hit her, and she died a hero and saved seventy-seven lives."

There was astounded silence around the table. Everyone stared at me, and I knew I'd gone too far with the details. "Or something like that," I finished weakly.

"Edna Halverson," Gramma said, pointing her knife at me. "That was the only Edna on the Schultz side of the family. She was a Bolls, from over by Maryville, before she married. You're right. They had that hundred acres of worthless timber up on Holstein Dip Road. Never did amount to a hill of beans, that side of the family."

"But she was a hero," I said, my face all shining with pride for Aunt Edna. She was mine, after all. "She saved all those lives."

"Nah." Gramma went back to sawing at her ham. "Edna didn't die in no train accident. She was stabbed to death."

My mouth fell open and my eyes bugged out.

"By who?" Everybody around the table was dead silent, even Delight.

"Not by who, by what." Gramma took an endless time chewing her bite of meat. "It was her hoopskirt that did her in. They had those narrow steel hoops in their skirts back then, and the way I hear tell, Edna's hoop busted and sprung out and stabbed her in the back of the knee. Died of blood poisoning."

Six

I was so disgusted with Aunt Edna I could hardly finish my peach pie with whipped cream. A guardian angel who lies through her teeth! Boy. Wasn't that just like me, to get a guardian angel—pardon me, spirit guide—who told fibs bigger than even GeorgeAnn told.

I lost all my respect for Aunt Edna, right then and there, and I made up my mind that no way was I going to let her tell me what to do with my love life. I was going to go after Aron Bodensteiner with every female wile I could whomp up, and she could just keep her sermons to herself.

As soon as the table was cleared I said to Cootie, "Let's go squirrel hunting, want to?"

He looked at me through one squinted eye. "You want to go squirrel hunting? With me?"

"Sure. You're my brother. Why wouldn't I want to go squirrel hunting with you?"

"Because I'm your brother," he said wisely. There's nothing more irritating than a wise eleven-year-old.

"I cheered for you yesterday when you were playing basketball, didn't I?" I said smoothly.

"Yeah." He couldn't argue that one.

"See, now that I'm thirteen I'm too old for all that childish sibling rivalry, Chuck." I threw in the *Chuck* for good measure. It's his real name. He had head lice in first grade and got the nickname Cootie, but he's always hated it. Well, can you blame him?

He looked at me for a while more, finally decided I wasn't kidding, and turned to yell, "Hey, Daddy, can we go squirrel hunting? Uncle Dean?"

Oh, no. That wasn't part of my plan. Cootie would be easy enough to ignore, once we made contact with Aron, but not a brother, a father, and an uncle.

Luck was with me. I'd have credited it to my guardian angel if I hadn't known better. Daddy looked at Uncle Dean, and they shook their heads.

"You kids go on if you want. We've got important things to take care of this afternoon." Then they went to work finding the ball game on television and opening beer cans and fighting over who got the big chair with the footstool.

"You kids be careful now," Uncle Dean yelled. "Take the four-ten and break it till you need it."

I let Cootie carry the shotgun, properly broken open over his arm so it couldn't go off accidentally and shoot us. He carried the gun but I led the way, across the heifer pasture, over the steel gate, and into the woods that adjoined the Bodensteiner timber.

Once we got on the main timber road and headed north, toward Bodensteiners', I dropped back behind Cootie, supposedly so he'd have a clear shot if he saw a squirrel, but really so I could let my mind spread out and dream.

The whole woods sloped downhill to our left, all the way to the edge of the river. It was a shallow, sand-bottom river that most years was barely deep enough to canoe in. Where it went through town, by the basketball bridge, town kids waded and messed around in the water in hot weather. Out here in the woods the river seemed deeper and a darker khaki green in color.

The road we walked along was just barely wide enough to drive a tractor or a pickup through and haul firewood out. It was carpeted about six inches thick with fallen leaves, all faded to a sort of purple-gray by now. Most of the trees were oaks, with some patches of white-barked poplar and some other patches of dark green cedar. There was one kind of oak that kept its purplish brown leaves till way into the winter, so the trees weren't completely bare naked, but still there were enough leaves on the ground that we couldn't walk silently like good hunters.

That was fine with me. I didn't want to have anything to do with murdering squirrels. As you may have guessed, I was after bigger game.

A couple of times Cootie froze and motioned me to be quiet, then raised the shotgun and blasted away at something moving in a tree. He never hit anything, but a huge old hawk started following us, way up over the trees, circling and making angry noises. Once we scared up three wild turkeys and sent them flying into a tree to hide from us. They made so much noise that it took five minutes to get my heart back down to normal speed.

"Wish we could shoot one of them," Cootie muttered.

"You do and the Conservation Commission would shoot you."

We passed the falling down barbed-wire fence that marked the end of Uncle Dean's land and the beginning of Aron's. My heart speeded up again and I moved up alongside Cootie, pretending to help him look for game.

And in a few minutes, just as if I actually had a cooperative guardian angel, there he was. *Game*.

He moved slowly along the road toward us, his shotgun over the crook of his arm, his eyes scanning tree branches for flicks of a squirrel's tail. He heard our crunching at the same time we spotted him, and we came together under a big, leafy old oak.

"Hey, Cootie," Aron said. "You doing any good?"

He looked at me but didn't say hi or anything, just kind of registered that I was there.

"Hi, Aron," I said.

Cootie shrugged and said, "Nah, spotted a couple of nice big grays, but I missed 'em."

"I heard your shots," Aron said, and aimed another look at me.

I eased over by the tree and started swinging on a vine. There's this vine of some kind that grows up oak trees. I don't know what kind it is because I'm not interested in stuff like that, but it's about an inch thick and has dead brown bark on it. I sort of swung on it with one hand, for something to be doing and also to make him think of Tarzan. Me being Jane, of course.

Cootie said, "Let's go together, should we? Let's go down where those pines are, along the river."

Aron was looking right at me by that time, not paying any attention to Cootie at all. His eyes were smoldering into mine. I could see he was getting the Tarzan message. His chest sort of swelled out, as much as a narrow chest can swell out. For a second there, I thought he was going to drop his

54

shotgun, pound himself on the chest and yell, "Ahh-eeah-eeah."

"Aron?" Cootie raised his voice. "I said, let's go down where those pines are along the river."

I looked deep into his eyes and he looked deep into mine . . . and then I fell on my face.

The vine ripped loose from the tree. It whipped out and got Aron around the neck.

He yelped, jumped back, flung his arms out. His gun went off. There was a loud squawk from up in the tree, and suddenly something huge and dark fell on me, smothering me, *killing me*.

It weighed a ton and it was all over my head, hot and soft and prickly and smothering the life out of me. I fought wildly.

Then, just as suddenly, it was gone and Aron was helping me up. He was laughing fit to kill, and so was Cootie. I wasn't.

The thing lay at our feet. It was a wild turkey, huge and brown and bloody and yucky and dead.

That thing had been on my head. Its blood was in my hair. Oh barf, oh gag, oh *yuck*!

"I'm going to get you for this," I yelled at Aunt Edna, because I knew she'd done this. I started slapping at my hair and my jacket, trying to get the yuck off.

"It wasn't Aron's fault," Cootie said, misunderstanding my curse.

"I know that," I said, more to Aron than to

Cootie. "I was talking to . . . fate. I know it was an accident."

Aron scowled down at the heap of feathers that had been a wild turkey hen, sacred bird of the Iowa Conservation Commission. He nudged it with his toe, and looked worried. Worried, slipping toward panic. I could see him thinking about losing his hunting license, paying a fine he couldn't afford, getting into all kinds of trouble with his folks. I could see Cootie and me not being allowed to go hunting out here again for fear of a worse accident with one of us as the dead turkey.

"Okay," I said, "here's what we better do. Get a shovel from your barn, Aron, and we'll bury the body someplace where mushroom hunters will never find her. Then all we have to do is swear ourselves to secrecy, and no one will ever know."

I had their attention now, and my highly organized mind was in gear. "Cootie, you stay here with the corpse, kick some leaves over her just in case somebody comes through here. It's too late in the season for ginseng hunters, but on a Sunday afternoon you can't ever tell who might decide to go walking in here. I'll go back with Aron. I'll have to wash the blood off before we can go home."

All of a sudden I didn't mind the yuck in my hair. I had Aron all to myself for maybe twenty minutes. While the guys were kicking leaves over the body, I looked up toward heaven and stuck my tongue out, real quick.

On the walk back to Aron's place I couldn't think of anything clever to say, so I just enjoyed walking beside him. We came out of the woods near the farm buildings. Luck was with us, no thanks to Aunt Edna. No one was outside to see us as Aron ducked into a barn and I dipped a hand into the icy water of a stock tank. Actually there was hardly any blood on me at all, when I got to looking, just a little smear on one shoulder and down the arm of my jacket.

I guess Aron couldn't think of anything clever to say either, or else he was too worried about his hunting license. Anyway, we didn't say anything most of the way back.

But just before we got in sight of Cootie, he stopped and rested the spade against the ground and looked me in the eye again. "You're okay, you know that?" he said.

"Thanks. It's nothing."

"No, you're really being a sport about all this. I mean, almost getting shot and dead turkeys falling out of trees and all that. You're good in a crisis."

And you're gorgeous, I wanted him to say.

We were looking into each other's eyes pretty heavy there for a minute. Then I got uneasy, wondering what Aunt Edna was about to do to break us up this time. I pulled my gaze away from his and walked on.

Cootie had been scouting locations for the burial and found a good one, way off the road and behind some gooseberry bushes where there weren't any big tree roots to dig through. The guys took turns digging, and then between them they carried the corpse and rolled her into her grave.

After they'd covered her over and scattered leaves to hide the fresh earth, we stood looking at each other.

I cleared my throat and said, "May her soul live happily forever, in turkey heaven."

"Amen," we all said together.

"And nobody tells anybody a single word about this," I went on, "or a terrible curse will come down on him."

They muttered their agreement, and I thought, The terrible curse should be that you get a guardian angel!

Seven

Somehow I wasn't surprised to see Aunt Edna in the kitchen. It was one-thirty in the morning and I was too hungry to get to sleep, so I'd come down for potato chips.

I turned the kitchen light on and there she was, wearing a long flannel nightgown, a braid of hair down her back. She stood in front of the stove, stirring something in a small pan, and the burner was glowing. It gave me a quick scare, knowing she could do things like turning stoves on.

"What are you doing, Aunt Edna?" I sounded crabby. I felt crabby.

"Making you a little snack, dear." She turned and smiled at me over her shoulder. "I knew you were hungry, so I thought I'd fix you a little warm milk. I hope you appreciate the effort, Dagmar. I didn't think I was ever going to get this cookstove going. I stuck lighted matches in every opening I could find, but nothing seemed to catch fire."

"It's an electric stove," I said in a low voice.

"Yes, well some of these modern conveniences are just more trouble than they're worth. It doesn't have any kind of decent firebox to it at all. No water reservoir on the back, nothing a stove should have."

I started to remind her that she could get all the hot water she wanted just by turning the faucet, but then I decided, what's the use of arguing with her.

"Well, I appreciate the effort, Aunt Edna, but you really shouldn't have bothered. I'll just get a can of Coke and the rest of this bag of sour cream and onion ripple chips, and take them . . ."

As I reached for the potato-chip bag, it slid away from my hand and scooted down the counter.

"Coke and potato chips," Aunt Edna snapped. "It's no wonder you have terrible skin, and, incidentally, you're getting a cavity in a lower left molar. I'd get that taken care of as soon as possible, dear. No, a nice glass of warm milk, that's what you need for a nighttime snack. You sit down there at the table. This will be ready in a jiffy."

Warm milk. My stomach rolled over and died at the thought.

"I can't even stand cold milk, much less warm.

60

Thank you very much," I said in my hardest voice, "but I'll just take a can of Coke and these . . ."

Again I reached for the potato chips and again they slid away from me, this time landing in the sink, under the faucet. I made a lunge, but I was too late. The faucet turned on and splashed water right into the partly opened potato-chip bag.

Oh, yuck, I thought. Wet potato chips. That was worse than warm milk. Mad but helpless for the moment, I sank into a chair by the table and stared down into the mug of steaming milk my SG served me.

"I wish I could give you a nice oatmeal cookie to go with it," Aunt Edna said, "but I couldn't find any oatmeal in the cupboard, and there wasn't time to bake a batch anyhow. Why don't I leave you a list of ingredients and you can get them for me, and I'll bake you some nice oatmeal cookies. But you'll have to get me some firewood to put in the oven. I couldn't find any."

I sighed and decided to change the subject. "Aunt Edna, that was you this afternoon, wasn't it? Out in Bodensteiners' timber? The vine, the dead turkey, all of that?"

She sat down across the table from me and pulled a square of crocheting from a pocket in her nightgown. Didn't those old-time women ever stop making things?

"Thomas's woods," she said. "When I was a girl that was Thomas's woods. Lovely blackberries in there around the end of July. Well, sometimes the middle of July if it was a hot year. I remember once we got enough blackberries out of Thomas's woods to make twenty gallons of blackberry ice cream for the Fourth of July picnic. Back then—"

"Who *cares!*" I snarled. I wanted to yell it, but didn't want to wake up Mom and Daddy in the downstairs bedroom. "Quit trying to dodge the issue. Were you or were you not out there with us this afternoon, and did you cause that accident?"

"My good gracious no, child. What a thing to accuse me of. Guns are for the menfolk."

"But you were there, right?"

"Drink up your milk like a good girl. Yes, of course I was there. What kind of SG would I be if I let you go off in the woods with two irresponsible boys with loaded guns? My stars and garters, child, give me some credit."

"You made that vine come loose."

"Yes. Yes, I did do that. I will admit that I loosened the vine, because things were getting a bit too intense between you and that boy, and of course that's what I'm here for, to protect you from yourself and others."

"Did you do the turkey?" I accused her.

"No, no, now, you can't blame me for that. The bird had flown up in that tree when it heard you coming. Wild turkeys do that all the time, you know that. You can't blame me for that part of it. That was purely an accident."

I gave her a long hard look, and she blushed and looked away from me, so I knew she was lying.

"And that's another thing," I said suddenly. "What was all that garbage you were feeding me about dying in a train accident, saving seventy-seven people's lives? None of that ever happened, did it?"

Her face puckered up, but she didn't answer.

"Did it, Aunt Edna? You made that whole thing up, didn't you? Gramma Schultz said you died of blood poisoning when your hoopskirt broke and stabbed you in the back of the knee."

Her face puckered up some more, and I thought she was going to start bawling on me. With a sigh that blew all the hair off my forehead, I said more softly, "You didn't have to tell me all that junk."

"Well," she said defensively, "how would you like going through eternity having people ask, 'How did you die, Edna?' and having to say, 'I was done in by my undergarments.' I mean, you just think about that, young lady. How would you like it?"

"You're right," I said, fighting for a straight face.

"Oh, dear, I hope Rudy hasn't been listening in. I wouldn't want him to know. . . ."

"You've got the hots for this Rudy, right?" I said. "And you fed him that line about being a big-shot hero and saving people's lives and all that?"

She hung her head and blushed.

"Listen, Aunt Edna, I'll make you a deal. You

63

butt out of my love life and I won't mess yours up, okay? Keep your hands off of Aron and me, and I won't tell Rudy your little secret."

For a minute she seemed to be considering the deal, then she sat up straighter and gave me a dirty look. "You couldn't tell Rudy. You have no way of contacting him."

I was hoping she wouldn't think of that.

Nothing much happened for the next few days. I took a makeup test in history and passed it. Shelly had a fight with Matthew, broke up with him, and then took him back, all in one afternoon. She'd started doing that just to prove to everybody that she could be mean to him and he'd come back for more.

Other than that, life was pretty quiet. I didn't hear from Aunt Edna, although I let the pink plastic radio play on after sign-off Monday and Tuesday nights just to see if she had anything to say. But I didn't venture down into the kitchen in the middle of the night again. One mug of warm milk was as far as I was willing to go to make her happy. It tasted awful. And I figured if she really did start trying to light fires in an electric oven and baking me cookies, it was going to be my fault when the house burned down.

So life was peaceful. Maybe just a little boring without her visits, but peaceful anyway. I found myself snacking on carrot sticks instead of potato chips and watching my posture, for fear of Aunt

Edna correcting me. Mom asked me if I was dieting. Aunt Dorothy remarked on how nice and straight I was standing these days. She said Neese should take lessons from me.

All of that made me feel good. I started weighing myself every morning and looking sideways in the hall mirror to admire my new posture. Maybe a guardian angel wasn't entirely a rotten thing to have, I thought.

Except.

Except for Aron, who was looking at me more and more in history and in the halls between classes. I had rerouted my trips between classrooms so my path crossed his three times in the mornings and twice in the afternoons. Maybe he was rerouting himself, too; I couldn't be sure. All I knew was that we were meeting a whole lot more than we used to, and we had good long looks right in each other's eyes, every time. It was the biggest thrill of my life.

Except.

Except for knowing that Aunt Edna was watching over me, just waiting to dump a locker on Aron or throttle me with a tree vine or drop a dead turkey on my head. I don't care what she said, I wasn't buying that bit about the turkey being an accident. If she'd lie about being creamed by a train, she'd lie about anything.

Then came Thursday. Thursday, November sixteenth, a major day in my life. All day, whenever

Aron and I looked at each other he seemed to be full of something he was about to say. Finally, on our last eye contact of the day, after sixth period and before we had to get on separate buses, he said it at last.

"Hey, Dagmar?"

I went over to him, nervously eyeing the row of lockers.

"You going to the game tomorrow night?" he asked, getting his tongue a little tangled as he spoke.

I panicked. If I said I was going, he might think I already had plans with somebody else. If I said I wasn't going, he might think I didn't want to. So I shrugged and smiled up at him hopefully.

"You want to go with me?"

There. He said it. He really truly said it. He asked me for a date! I couldn't believe it. My very first date-asking. Thursday, November sixteenth, 3:50 P.M.

"Well, do you want to go or not?" he said, looking nervous about my hesitation.

Deftly I moved around beside him and propped my hand against the door of his locker, just in case its toggle bolts got suddenly loosened.

"Sure," I said. Then I remembered. "But my dad won't let me go out on dates alone or with anyone or in a car. He'd have to drive us and bring us home." I held my breath.

Aron looked relieved. "That's okay. I wasn't sure how I was going to get us there anyhow."

I went home singing and tap dancing all the way. Daddy was off driving a load of hogs to the sale barn. He helped out sometimes when they needed truck drivers on sale nights. Thursday nights they had hog sales, and two Friday nights a month they had cattle sales, and the first Saturday night of the month were horse sales. . . . Why am I telling you this? I'm getting to be as bad as Aunt Edna. Feel free to yell "Who *cares*" at me if I get off the subject.

I told Mom about Aron asking me to the game, and she said ask Daddy; I knew she'd say that.

When he got home around eight, I told him and asked him, and he said fine, he and Cootie were going to the game anyway, we could just pick up Aron on our way.

Well, what can I say? Not a dream date maybe, Daddy and Cootie and the pickup truck. But still, my first date.

I didn't listen to the radio that night in bed. I didn't want to hear from Aunt Edna. All I wanted to do was decide what to wear and how to fix my hair and how much eye makeup I could get away with.

Eight

She was in the bathroom with me the whole time I was taking my bath and drying my hair. She kept her back turned to me while I was naked, which I thought was very nice considering the fact that she could see me naked any time she wanted to, being an angel.

"Young girls never listen to the warnings of their elders," she said in a testy voice.

"Well, you're my elder, that's for sure," I muttered as I stepped out of the tub and started drying.

"Young girls always think they know best," Aunt Edna said, harder and louder. "I've done everything I could to keep you from getting involved with this boy, at your age, and you're just too stubborn to listen to my good advice."

"Your advice was no boyfriends till I was twenty years old."

"That's right, and with a girl as headstrong as you are, I'm not at all sure twenty will be old enough. Thirty might be more like it."

I turned the hair dryer on and drowned her out. She unplugged it.

"Listen to me when I'm talking to you, Dagmar. If I let you get into trouble with this boy, kissing and that sort of thing, how am I going to explain it to Rudy? I mean, this is my first SG assignment. The committee is going to be watching very closely to make sure I don't fail with you. They kept me on Level Two for, what, ninety-five years I believe it was. Let's see, I moved on from earth in eighteen ninety-six, or was it seven? No no, I'm right, it was ninety-six because Bob—that was our oldest boy—he graduated from high school in—"

"Who ca—"

"Yes, yes, I know, dear. All I'm saying is that it took me quite a while to get promoted to Level Three, nearly a hundred years, and you don't get to be an SG until—oh my, I'm talking too much, aren't I?"

She plugged the hair dryer in again. I turned it off and said, "Tell me about all this Level Two and Level Three business. I'm curious."

"Well, of course you are, dear. Everyone down here on Level One is curious about what happens after they . . . pass over. That's only natural. Where would all the hundreds of religions be if they couldn't all claim that they had the key to everlasting life? I mean, stop and think about it. That's their main selling point, isn't it?"

"I wouldn't know. I'm always playing hangman with Cootie during the sermons."

She turned to look at me, since I was decently wrapped in a towel, and her eyes met mine with a sudden gleam.

"I used to play dots in church. Do you know that one? You draw a grid of dots, ten across and ten down, and take turns drawing a line from dot to dot, and whoever can draw the final line to enclose a square gets to put his initial in it and take another turn, and the one with the most initials in boxes at the end wins. Do you know that one?"

"No, but it sounds like fun." I don't know why, but I suddenly felt like grinning at her. Probably just the excitement of my first date.

"Meet us back here at the truck as soon as the game's over," Daddy said. Then he dragged Cootie off across the parking lot and left me and Aron to walk into the high-school building alone together. He's a good sport.

It was like making a grand entrance at the ball, almost, walking into that school beside Aron. It was wonderful! Everybody looked at us and made mental notes to tell other people that Aron Bodensteiner had brought Dagmar Schultz to the game Friday night.

Red faced but proud, we climbed the bleachers in the cheering section and stepped across feet and legs till we could sit down. Daddy and Cootie were clear down at the other end where we didn't have to see them at all. Who knew where Aunt Edna was, but I'd made up my mind to forget about her. She wasn't going to mess this up for me.

It was the first varsity basketball games of the season, first the girls' game, which had already started when we got there, and then the boys' game after that. Us against Colesburg. So far their girls were creaming ours, but I couldn't have cared less. To me, the whole point of basketball games was who you might meet or talk to or sit by in the bleachers.

All through the rest of the girls' game and the first half of the boys', Aron kept his eyes on the court action, but I could tell he was thinking about me as much as I was thinking about him. Well, almost as much. His attention got away from me at free-throw time, or when our team got down close to their basket, or when either side scored. Or when any of his friends yelled at him. But other than that, his mind was right on me every minute.

At halftime in the second game, we went across the legs and feet, down the bleachers, and out into the main hallway where the vendors were selling popcorn and candy and pop. Aron offered me anything I wanted, but I just took a small Coke. For one thing, I didn't want mysterious forces knocking a popcorn bag out of my hands.

For another thing, I was planning ahead. What I really *really* wanted was for him to kiss me, and the only way that was going to happen was by my getting him off alone somewhere during this last half of the game. Off alone, away from distractions and other kids and teachers patrolling the halls. Away from Daddy and Cootie, and especially away from my heavenly helper.

We could dodge all but one of them without too much trouble. Any couple of kids who want to be alone together to mess around can always manage to duck teachers, parents, brothers, and other kids. Aunt Edna was going to be the tricky one.

While we were still standing in front of the trophy case in the hallway, eating and drinking, the game started up again and everybody else wandered back down the hall and into the gym.

"You want to go back?" Aron asked.

I couldn't tell for sure if he wanted to watch the rest of the game, or if his mind was running in the same track as mine was. But, no guts, no glory, right? I decided to take the plunge.

"I don't really want to go back in, unless you do," I said, sort of smiling up through my hair. He got the message.

His face turned kind of red and he said, "What would you rather do?"

"I don't know. What would you rather do?"

He hesitated for a long time, as if he was telling himself No guts, no glory, too. Then he leaned down close and said, "Kiss you."

The thrill of that almost knocked me right off my legs. I was about to get my first kiss.

If.

If only I could figure out some place we could go, where Aunt Edna wouldn't follow, because sure as the world, if there was any way for her to screw this up for me, she was going to do it.

Where, where, where? My steel-trap mind ran over all the possibilities. Outside in the pickup in the parking lot? No, she'd be there. She'd probably turn the ignition on and run us into somebody's brand-new car.

Over in the school yard under the big elm trees? Heck no! No more standing under trees. No more dead birds falling on me!

Someplace in the building . . . think fast, Dagmar. Where would Aunt Edna not go?

Aha! I had it.

"Come with me," I said in a dark, mysterious voice. I took Aron's hand and led him to our destiny.

Nine

"The boys' rest room?" Aron said, puzzled, as we slowed to a stop in front of a door in the third-floor hallway. "The *boys'* rest room? Wow, Dagmar, you are one kinky woman, you know that?"

He looked down at me with a new gleam in his eyes.

"Don't ask questions," I commanded, and pulled him through the door.

Of course, telling somebody not to ask questions is like telling them not to smile. As soon as you say it, they have to do what you told them not to.

"Not that I'm complaining," he said, "but what are we doing up here in the third-floor boys' room, Dagmar? Hiding from somebody? I mean, besides teachers and other kids and your dad and Cootie?"

74

"Isn't that enough to be hiding from?" I sure wasn't about to tell him we were really trying to dodge an elderly spirit guide who dropped lockers and dead turkeys on people. And died from being attacked by her underwear. And didn't believe in young love under the age of twenty.

The third-floor boys' rest room was one of my greatest ideas, actually. Nobody in the building was going to come all the way up here to use the rest room, and Aunt Edna sure wouldn't come into a boys', not if she was too modest to look at me in the bathtub at home.

At last, alone together. The room was almost dark, with just a little moonlight coming in from a high window behind the toilet stalls. Moonlight . . . romance. Ah. All we had to do was block out of our minds all that embarrassing plumbing along the wall there, and we had a perfect setting for my first kiss.

Aron looked down at me and sort of smiled. "You are sure different from any girl I've ever known, Dagmar. You're . . . exciting."

He didn't know the half of it.

I tipped my head back and closed my eyes and puckered up.

He moved in closer and put his arms around me.

The door lock clicked.

We jumped apart! "What was that?" we whispered together.

We froze and listened for steps or breathing outside the door, but there wasn't any. No one was out there. Aron tried the door handle.

Locked.

We were locked in.

We were *locked in* the third-floor boys' room at ten o'clock on a Friday night, where no one would find us till Monday morning when we'd be dead.

"Whose stupid idea was this, to come up here?" I wailed.

Aron looked at me.

I pulled myself together. "Yes, well, uh, okay. So the door lock went off accidentally and we're trapped in here. So. How bad could it be? I don't suppose you know how to pick locks?"

He gave me a long, level look, as though he suspected me of knowing more than I was saying. "It didn't just lock itself, Dagmar."

I shrugged and looked as dumb as possible. Darkness helped. We could see the outlines of each other's faces, but I was pretty sure he couldn't read anything in my eyes that would give me away.

"You know what it must have been?" I said suddenly. "Cootie. He must have followed us up here, tiptoed up, locked the door for a joke, and snuck away. Or else he's hiding out there laughing. *Cootie!*" I bellowed through the door.

"Get over here and unlock this door so I can kill you, Cootie," Aron hollered.

Nothing. Distant voices cheering a score. No

shuffling feet in our hallway. No giggling little rat face.

Of course, I knew there wouldn't be. I knew darn good and well who locked us in here, and the minute I told Aron about her, it would be the end of my love life forever. First he'd laugh himself silly, then he'd decide I had serious head problems, then he'd tell everyone in the whole school, and Aunt Edna would get her wish. I would be twenty or maybe thirty before any boy would get this close to me again, if ever—maybe never.

I wanted to bawl. Or punch Aunt Edna out. Or die, but then I'd have to spend eternity with the old bat on Level Three, wherever that was. And a hundred years from now I'd be making up wild stories about how I died, because I couldn't admit to my guidee that I died of embarrassment at being locked in a boys' room at a basketball game on my first date.

I suddenly had a little surge of fellow-feeling for Aunt Edna, for making up the train story. I hated her guts for locking us in, but at the same time, I could begin to see a family trait, handed down through the ages—Schultz women doing stupid embarrassing things and lying to cover up.

"We gotta get out of here," Aron said. He felt around for the light switch and turned it on. Goodbye romance, hello toilets.

We looked around hopelessly.

"That window," I said.

It was small and high up, over one of the toilet stalls.

"Third floor," Aron reminded me.

"I know, but maybe there's a roof under it or something. There always is in the movies. I'll just climb up there and take a look. Give me a hand."

We crowded into the stall and I stood carefully on the toilet seat, one foot on each side. I could see out the window, but not far enough.

Bracing one hand on Aron's head, I raised my foot to the top of the toilet tank and started to ease up.

Suddenly an invisible force hit the side of my other leg. The foot on the toilet seat slipped off and down, into the cold water below.

And jammed there.

All of my weight coming down on that one foot drove it right into the throat of that toilet bowl and jammed it there. Thank you, Edna and the heavenly host, thank you very much!

Aron had caught the top of me when I fell and sort of stood me up on my other leg.

"Ouch-ouch-ouch," I yelled. "Don't twist me, you'll break my leg."

"Hang onto me, I'll get you out," he said, suddenly brave and strong.

I stood there like a pelican on one foot, hanging on to the back of his shirt collar with one hand and the toilet-paper dispenser with the other, while he bent over and tried to work my foot loose. Above his back I looked upward and spoke silently to Aunt Edna, hoping she would read my lips.

"Get me out of here, or I'll tell Rudy about your hoopskirt."

Nothing.

"Get me out of here, and I promise to be good. No boyfriends till I'm twenty."

Nothing.

"Get me out of here, or I'll kill you!"

A stupid threat, considering.

My foot was beginning to hurt. It felt as if it was swelling around the ankle.

"Please, Aunt Edna?" I whimpered, and that time I forgot to keep it silent.

Aron grunted, "Aunt Edna? What are you talking about?"

I patted his shoulder. "That's just my little pet name for you."

He twisted around to look at me. "Aunt *Edna*? Boy, Dagmar, you are—"

"An original?" I offered hopefully.

He grinned. Then he stopped grinning. "Your foot is really stuck in there. I can't get it out. We're going to have to get help."

"Fine. Wonderful. Just run out through that locked door and get the janitor. I'll wait here," I added nastily.

For a minute we glared at each other, then my face cracked and his face cracked and we broke up laughing.

Then suddenly we weren't laughing anymore, we were gazing deep into each other's eyes. With a little twisting and shuffling Aron got around to the front side of me and put his arms around me.

Here comes my first kiss, I thought with wild happiness.

And it did. And it was wonderful for about half a minute.

Then we both broke up laughing at the circumstances, and the romantic mood went right down the tubes. So to speak.

Ten

We started yelling in earnest then, and Aron took off one of his boots and banged the water pipe under the sink with it for about ten minutes.

Then, suddenly, the door opened and in came Hershey, the main janitor. His name was Hershall, but we called him Hershey. He was a big old guy with a totally bald head and no sense of humor whatever.

"Heard a racket in the pipes," he said. We knew he was always in the building on game nights, and we'd hoped he would be sitting in his room among the basement pipes, not up in the gym watching the game.

"The door got locked accidentally," Aron explained. "And then she was trying to see if we could get out . . . the . . . window . . ."

Explanations were lost on Hershey. He didn't give a fat rat. He just looked at us as if he not only suspected the worst, he knew it. You could just see "sex, booze, drugs" parading through his mind as he looked at us.

"Can you just get my foot out, Hershey?" I said impatiently.

He grunted, set down his tool case, and crowded into the stall with me. Muttering something I couldn't hear and didn't want to, he slipped his hand into the water, untied my tennis shoe, and levered my foot out of shoe, water, and toilet.

"Yay," Aron and I yelled together.

Hershey just gave us a long dark look, picked up his tools, and stood in the doorway until we exited the rest room.

I tried buttering him up. "That was really clever of you, untying my shoe. How did you think of it?"

His face took on a don't-pull-that-garbage-on-me expression. "I been a school janitor thirty-seven years now. You think you're the first airhead to get a foot caught in a toilet in thirty-seven years? The stupid tricks I've seen . . ." He shook his head. Then, pointedly, he locked the rest room door behind us and clomped on down the hall.

Aron held me up while I forced the sopping shoe back onto my foot and tied the soaked laces. The foot wasn't really hurt. I could hobble along on it pretty well.

Good thing, too, because just then the final cheer went up, and we could hear the rattle-squeak of the bleachers as everybody climbed down and headed for the door.

We met Daddy and Cootie by the front door as the last of the crowd flowed out toward the parking lot.

Daddy, of course, spotted the limp and the shoe. "What happened to your foot? Your shoe's all wet."

I shook my head. "You don't want to know," I said.

He looked at me for a long minute, then accepted that statement. I never appreciated him more in my life than I did right then.

"This concludes our broadcast day from Radio Station KADR, Elkader, Iowa, in the heart of the hill country," the radio announcer said. I was lying in bed with the pink radio plugged into my ears and a cold, wet towel pinned around my ankle to keep the swelling down.

I waited grimly through the announcer's sign-off stuff about watts or whatever. The next voice I hear, I thought, better be Aunt Edna.

A few minutes of static, and there she was. "That was very naughty of you, dear. What you did tonight. If I'd gone into a boys' outhouse with a young man, I'd have had to marry him."

Her words were about what I expected, but for some reason her voice didn't match them. Her voice sounded sort of, well, high and happy. Almost giddy.

"You sound disgustingly cheerful for someone who just ruined someone else's love life," I snarled.

"Now now, dear. You mustn't exaggerate. Your young man was smiling at you very warmly, I thought, when you said good-night."

Well, that was true. "That's true," I said, "but that doesn't make it any better, what you did to us. Locking us in that rest room, and then knocking my foot off the toilet seat. What the heck kind of guardian angel would do such a thing? What would Rudy think of you, Aunt Edna? Don't you guys up there on Level Three have any code of ethics?"

To my amazement she started to giggle. Have you ever heard a hundred-and-forty-year-old dead woman giggle? No, scratch that question. Of course you haven't. You'll have to take my word for it. It's weird.

"What's gotten into you tonight, Aunt Edna? You sound as if you swallowed the feather."

"I don't know what that means, dear. But yes, I suppose I do sound a little, well . . ."

"Silly," I said flatly.

"Oh, Dagmar, you're so naughty."

I clenched my teeth. This new kittenish Aunt

Edna was worse than the old one. She was acting like . . . oh, no.

"Aunt Edna, did something happen between you and Rudy?"

She giggled again. Heaven help us, I thought. No, no! Scratch that wish!

"What happened?" I asked darkly.

"Well, I expect I have you to thank, dear. You see, Rudy was monitoring me while I was monitoring you. Part of his job, don't you know. And when your young man kissed you there in the—well, never mind where—Rudy happened to be monitoring me at the time, and he sort of, well . . ." She giggled again.

"Got turned on?"

"Became romantically inclined," she corrected me. "Isn't love grand?"

"I wouldn't know," I said pointedly. "Somebody keeps interfering in my love life. Remember?"

She sighed a dreamy sigh. "Yes, well, I am sorry about that, Dagmar, dear. I can see now that I was wrong to try to stand in your way. You seem to be a capable young lady for someone so headstrong, and I'm sure Aron is an honorable lad. From now on I intend to do everything I can to help you along love's flower-strewn path."

From behind her I thought I heard a low masculine chuckle. Then she giggled again and said, "Stop it, Rudy. I'm talking to Dagmar. Stop it, you naughty man." And she giggled again.

"You're going to *help* me with my love life," I said.

"Yes, dear."

I sighed a very long hopeless sigh and turned the radio off.

Where did I ever get the idea that being thirteen was going to make life less complicated?